Jack Russell:

DOG DETECTIVE

Muddy Mystery

I ate my way along a trail of biscuits, and in behind a bale of hay. I was really getting into this undercover work…

Splot.

Suddenly I was under cover all right – under cover of a bucket of mud.

Also available in this series:

Dognapped!
Pug in Trouble
Beware of the Postman

Jack Russell:

DOG DETECTIVE

Muddy Mystery

Darrel & Sally Odgers

SCHOLASTIC

Scholastic Children's Books
Euston House, 24 Eversholt Street,
London, NW1 1DB, UK
A division of Scholastic Ltd
London ~ New York ~ Toronto ~ Sydney ~ Auckland
Mexico City ~ New Delhi ~ Hong Kong

First published in Australia by Scholastic Australia Pty Ltd, 2005
This edition published in the UK by Scholastic Ltd, 2006

10 digit ISBN 0 439 94288 8
13 digit ISBN 978 0439 94288 1

Printed in the UK by CPI Bookmarque, Croydon, CR0 4TD

10 9 8 7 6 5 4

Dear Readers,

The story you're about to read is about me and my friends, and how we solved the case of the Phantom Mudder. To save time, I'll introduce us all to you now. Of course, if you know us already, you can skip ahead to Chapter One.

I am Jack Russell, Dog Detective. I live with my landlord, Sarge, in Doggeroo. Sarge detects human-type crimes. I detect important crimes. Those are the ones that deal with dogs! I'm a Jack Russell terrier, so I am dogged and intelligent.

Next door to Sarge and me live Auntie Tidge and Foxie. Auntie Tidge is lovely. She has biscuits. Foxie is not

lovely. He's a fox terrier (more or less).
He used to be a street dog, and a thief,
but he's reformed now. Auntie Tidge
has even got rid of his fleas. Foxie
sometimes helps me with my cases.

Uptown Lord Setter (Lord Red for
short) lives in Uptown House with
Caterina Smith. Lord Red means well.
He tries to help with my cases, but he
sometimes gets overexcited.

That's all you need to know, so let's
get on with Chapter One.

Yours doggedly,

Jack Russell – the detective with a nose
for crime.

 Mud

One wet Friday, Sarge told me about the Doggeroo Dog Show.

"It's been going for a hundred and fifty years, Jack," Sarge said. "It's one of the oldest dog shows in Australia."

I wagged my tail. I like to please Sarge.

"I'm working there as a steward," said Sarge. "What do you think, Jack? Want to come to a dog show tomorrow?"

I snorted. That's what I think of dog shows.

"Great," said Sarge. "You can come."

Jack's Facts.

Dogs understand what humans say.
*Humans **think** they understand what*
dogs say.
Therefore, dogs are smarter than humans.
This is a fact.

That afternoon, Foxie and I dug a big hole near the apple tree.

Most dogs won't let another dog help bury a bone, but I'm not like that.

I know, and Foxie knows, that my garden is my **terrier-tory**. That means no dog can come into the garden without my permission.

"It's very muddy, Jack," said Foxie, when we finished the hole. "I've got mud all over my paws."

"Who cares?" I dropped the bone into the hole and started to push the mud on top of it with my nose. "Mud's good."

"Foxie! Foxie-woxie!" Auntie Tidge was calling Foxie home.

I laughed. "I bet she wants to bath you."

"Auntie Tidge would never **terriorise** me that way," said Foxie. "She will just wipe the mud off my paws."

"Foxie-woxie!"

"Coming!" yapped Foxie, and took off through the hedge.

I walked over the top of my buried bone to firm the mud down. While I did that, I made a quick **nose map**.

Jack's map. . .

1. Mud everywhere.

2. The buried beef bone.

3. A place under the tree where
a cat sat last Thursday.

I waited a while. *Sniff-sniff*. Then I
smelled the smell I expected to smell...

4. Flowery soap, mixed with wet dog.
I heard Foxie's voice faintly howling.
"I'll get you for this, Jack Russell!"
Told you so, I thought.
"Jackie-wackie?" That was Auntie
Tidge calling me. I love Auntie Tidge, so I
crawled through the hedge, and raced
round the corner, wagging my tail.
"How's my dear Jack?" Auntie Tidge

bent down to pat me.

I **jack-jumped** up and knocked her glasses sideways so I could give her a big lick on the nose. She loves it when I do that.

Auntie Tidge caught me. "Bath time, Jack," said Auntie Tidge.

Traitor.

Jack's Glossary

Terrier-tory. *Territory owned by a terrier.*

Terriorise. *Frighten.*

Nose map. *Way of storing information collected by the nose.*

Jack-jump. *A sudden spring by a Jack.*

 # Smelling Soap

The next morning, we went to the show with Sarge and Auntie Tidge.

I stuck my head out the window.

<u>Jack's Facts.</u>

Dogs have noses. Cars have windows.
One must be stuck out the other.
This is a fact.

I sneezed. "Everything smells like soap," I complained to Foxie.

"*You* smell like soap, Jack Russell," growled Foxie.

Doggeroo Showground was wet and muddy. Auntie Tidge carried us inside the pavilion. "You go and play, darlings, while I find my friend Dora," said Auntie Tidge.

The dogs inside the pavilion all smelled like soap, especially Lord Red, who lives at Uptown House with Caterina Smith. He was racing in circles, whirling his tail. He didn't even notice Foxie and me.

"Lordie, *Lordie!*" yelled Caterina Smith. "Have you got muddy paws?"

Red ran faster.

"There's that stupid setter running loose again," said a man with three bone-heads on leads. "It shouldn't be allowed."

"The steward tried to ban *my* dog last year for bad behaviour," said a man with grey mud on his boots. He was holding a bonehead wearing a muzzle. "He should have banned the setter."

"Your dog bit the judge's wife," the three-boneheads man pointed out.

"She got in the way. That setter is about to – watch out!"

There was a scream from over near the door.

Lord Red had **greeted** a woman who was wearing high-heeled shoes.

"Lordie, *Lordie*, come here!" yelled Caterina Smith. She pulled Red away.

High Heels stamped her foot. Red yelped, and tucked his tail between his legs.

"Oops," said High Heels. "I must have trodden on his tail."

"Let me sponge your coat," said Caterina Smith. "A bit of soap will fix it."

High Heels pushed her away. "Never mind. Dogs will be dogs."

"Lord Red does get so excited," said Caterina Smith. "I hope your coat will be all right."

"What's a bit of mud on a brand new coat?" said High Heels. "At the show last week a spaniel chewed the heels right off my new shoes, and the week before, a bulldog ate my gold lipstick. And last year in this very pavilion I was—"

"Did it make the bulldog sick?" interrupted Caterina Smith.

"What? Oh no. The *bulldog* was just fine."

"That's the main thing, isn't it?" said Caterina Smith. "Oops!" she added, as Red tried to greet the woman again. "Better go!" She led Red away.

High Heels stared after them. Then she marched off. Foxie and I jumped out of her way, just in time, and one of the boneheads growled at us.

"I see terrier toothpicks."

Foxie and I didn't want to be forced to hurt the bonehead, so we left.

There were dogs everywhere. The

three squekes who live on the corner were yaffling about, doing what squekes do.

Shuffle, the pug who lives near the reserve, was sulking in his basket. "I don't like dog shows," he snuffled crossly.

Polly, the dachshund from over the river, was **daching** about with her person, Gloria Smote. Jill Russell from near the station was guarding a bone in the corner. Jill always pokes me with her nose, but she's a real **ace**!

<u>Jack's Facts.</u>

Jack is a male name.
Jill is a female name.

Therefore, a female Jack Russell is really a
Jill Russell.
This is a fact.

All these dogs smelled of soap. I
sneezed.

Jack's Glossary

Greet. *This is done by rising to*
the hind legs and clutching a
person with the paws while
slurping them up the face.

Daching. *The way dachshunds*
move about.

Ace. *Great, fine, the very best.*

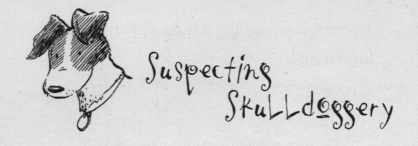

Suspecting Skullduggery

I was still sneezing when Lord Red raced up.

"Jack! Jack!" he barked. His whirling tail sent two Shih tzus scampering. "What's going down, Jack?"

"You're racing about, scaring Shih tzus," I said.

"Who's being dognapped? Who's stealing balls? Who's doing bad things?"

Ever since I solved the case of the Doggeroo Dognapping Mystery, Lord Red has been hoping I'll let him help detect something.

"You're the one doing bad things," I said. "Why did you greet that High Heels woman?"

"Because she came with the biscuit man," said Red. "I like the biscuit man. Caterina Smith says he might give me a ribbon."

Foxie pricked up his ears. "What biscuit man? Where?" (Foxie loves biscuits.)

"The biscuit man is the judge," said Red. "He smells of biscuits. My tail hurts, Jack. Do you think I can win a ribbon with a sore tail? Will you investigate, Jack?"

"Don't be silly," I said. "I investigate **skulldoggery**, not sore tails."

Red got down on his elbows and stuck his tail in the air. "If I see any skulldoggery, can I come and tell you, Jack?"

"Of course," I said. "Jack Russell's the name, detection's the game."

Red was really pleased.

"Lordie, *Lordie!*"

"Caterina Smith is calling," said Red. "See you later, Jack." He trotted off.

Foxie sniffed the air. "I'm going to find Auntie Tidge and get a **special biscuit.**"

After Foxie had gone, I looked for Sarge. On the way, I saw High Heels. She had a smeary wet patch on her coat. She was talking to the man who smelled of biscuits.

"Are you enjoying this show, Katya?" asked Biscuits.

"Oh yes," said High Heels. "All these lovely, clean, shiny dogs. . ."

Biscuits smiled, and patted her on the shoulder.

"Although one *did* put mud all over my new coat," she continued.

"I expect it was that setter of Caterina Smith's," said Biscuits. "He's a lovely dog, and completely harmless."

"A lovely dog!" agreed the woman. "Could you give me a show schedule, dear? I like to keep up with which class comes next."

"Here you are, dear." Biscuits took a booklet out of his pocket and gave it to her.

High Heels clicked her fingers at me. "Who's a sweet little doggie, then?"

I sniffed and walked away. I was offended.

Jack's Facts.

A Jack Russell may be sweet.
A Jack Russell may be little.
*A Jack Russell is **never** a 'sweet little doggie'.*
This is a fact.

Just then, I saw the boneheads man again. He was talking to Sarge in a loud, rough voice.

"Now, look here!" he said.

Immediately, I suspected skulldoggery.

"No, you look here, Mr Latiman," said Sarge. "You can't show those dogs today."

"And why not?" Mr Latiman moved a step closer.

"Back off," I growled. My hackles rose. This looked like a case for Jack Russell, Dog Detective!

"Entries closed two weeks ago," said Sarge. "Rules are rules. Take your dogs home, Mr Latiman."

Mr Latiman snarled. "You'll be sorry you took this attitude, Sergeant Russell!"

I growled, to show the man that Sarge was protected by a capable **doggyguard**.

"Back off, Jack," rumbled one of the

boneheads. "You smell like soap."

I didn't want to be forced to hurt the boneheads, so I went back to Foxie and Auntie Tidge. The smell of soap and shampoo and Pooch Polish and chew toys and wet dog and mud was getting stronger every minute.

Lord Red bounded up. "Jack, Jack, I've found some skulldoggery! Will you investigate, Jack?"

"That depends," I said. "What kind of skulldoggery?"

"Someone has **mudded** Shuffle the pug," barked Red. "Shuffle the pug was clean, now he is all mudded. Isn't that skulldoggery, Jack?"

"No," I said. "That's just natural."

Jack's Glossary

Skulldoggery. *Wicked goings on that concern dogs.*

Special biscuits. *Auntie Tidge makes these. They don't harm terrier teeth.*

Doggyguard. *A bodyguard who is a dog.*

Mudded. *Being covered or splattered with mud.*

Soggy Doggy

"Welcome to the one-hundred-and-fiftieth Doggeroo Dog Show!" howled a **loudhowler**. "A special welcome to Judge Gibbs, and to our new steward, Sergeant Russell."

No-one took any notice, so the loudhowler howled it again, louder. Lots of dogs howled back.

<u>Jack's Facts.</u>

When a howler howls, polite dogs howl back.
This is a fact.

"First class – spaniels!" howled the loudhowler.

"What a pity it's so muddy today," Auntie Tidge said to Dora Barkins, as the spaniels entered the ring. The man who smelled of biscuits was waiting for them in the centre. "That pug looks as if he's been rolling in mud," said Dora, staring at Shuffle.

The spaniels were going in circles around Judge Gibbs, while Sarge ticked off numbers on his clipboard. Soon, the judge tied a ribbon to one of the collars.

"Second class – dachshunds," howled the loudhowler, as the spaniels left the ring.

The dachshunds dached towards the ring and began to trot round in circles. I was surprised to see that Polly wasn't with them.

"Where's Polly?" I wondered aloud to Foxie.

"Maybe she's been **dognapped**," suggested Foxie.

"In that case," I said, "I'll need to investigate."

Foxie sniffed and pricked his ears. "I smell biscuits. Do you hear a biscuit bag, Jack?"

Just then, Gloria Smote rushed up with Polly on a lead. Polly was dripping all over the place. She was a very soggy doggy.

"Why is your dog wet, Gloria?" asked Sarge.

"I washed her," explained Gloria Smote.

"You should have washed her earlier,"

said Sarge. "You can't show wet dogs."

Gloria's eyes looked as red as a white rabbit's. "I did wash her earlier. Just before her class I found her covered in mud. I had to wash her again."

"Rules are rules," Sarge said. "You can't show Polly in the dachshund class, Gloria. Tell you what, why not transfer her entry to the small dog class?"

Gloria smiled. She has little white teeth just like Polly's. "Oh, Sergeant Russell, you are clever! I'll go and dry her now."

I decided I liked Gloria Smote.

Foxie and I went to help by licking Polly dry. Polly smelled of soap and biscuits.

"Stop that!" said Gloria Smote. "I don't want dog slobber all over Polly!"

I decided I didn't like Gloria Smote.

As Foxie and I retreated, Lord Red dashed up, whirring his tail. "Jack, Jack! I've found some more skulldoggery!"

"What is it this time, Red?" I asked.

"Somebody mudded Polly!" said Red. "That's skulldoggery, isn't it?"

I was about to remind Red that mud was not skulldoggery, when I thought again. If someone had mudded Shuffle *and* Polly, maybe there really *was* skulldoggery afoot.

I couldn't investigate the case at once, because Muddy Boots and his bonehead were bullying Sarge. This called for Sarge's doggyguard – me.

I snarled.

The bonehead growled.

Muddy Boots kicked me away. "Give

me a number, steward! I'm going to show my dog. I paid my entry fee two weeks ago."

"And I paid it back," said Sarge. "You were banned from the last show, Mr Bootle. You are not allowed to show that dog. It bites."

"I was framed!" snapped Muddy Boots. "It wasn't my fault my dog bit that woman! Some dogs bite. What can you do?"

"Rules are rules," said Sarge.

Muddy Boots sneered. "You made an exception for that dripping dachshund."

"That's different," said Sarge. "You can't show your dog today, Mr Bootle. And don't come next year, either."

Muddy Boots pointed at Sarge. "You'll be sorry you said that!"

"I doubt it," said Sarge. "And don't
you ever kick my dog again!" He bent to
rub my ears. "OK, Jack?"

"Third class – Dalmatians!" howled
the loudhowler.

Five black dogs came towards us, led
by angry people.

"No, no," said Sarge. "This is the Dalmatian class, not the black labrador class."

"We *are* the Dalmatian class!" snapped one woman.

Sarge frowned. "Surely Dalmatians have spots?"

"They *have* got spots!' said a man. "Someone's covered our dogs with mud."

We looked. I sniffed. I could smell mud, and soap . . . and something else. I sneezed. My superior **super-sniffer** still wasn't working very well.

"You can't show muddy dogs," said Sarge.

The loudhowler called the schnauzer class instead.

Four people came up with schnauzers. Sarge ticked them off on his clipboard. "Where are the other two?" he asked. "I have six entries here."

"Here," said Mr Crisp. "Someone's put mud over my dogs! Just *look* at them!"

Sarge and I looked at the mudded schnauzers.

"This is getting ridiculous!" said Sarge. "Go and wash them." He borrowed the loudhowler. "Attention everyone! *Please* control your dogs! Muddy dogs may *not* be shown!"

Mr Crisp went away, and the rest of the class trotted into the ring.

Lord Red came bounding up. "Are you going to investigate, Jack? Are you?"

"Yes," I said. "Jack Russell's the name, detection's the game. I already have some suspects."

Jack's Glossary

Loudhowler. *A thing dog shows have so people and dogs can hear instructions.*

Dognapped. *Kidnapping done to a dog.*

Super-sniffer. *Jack's nose in super-tracking mode.*

The Phantom Mudder Strikes Again

"What can I do, Jack?" Lord Red was prancing about.

"You find out how many dogs have been mudded," I said.

Red ran off, and I heard him barking out questions. I trotted off to interview my first suspect.

Polly was sitting in a cage with a blanket over the top. I poked my superior super-sniffer through the folds. I sniffed. I could still smell soap, but when I got closer, I could also detect damp dog and biscuit and Foxie slobber.

Polly glared at me. "Go away, Jack Russell. Gloria Smote will be cross if you lick my face again."

"It isn't *my* fault you got mudded!" I said. I looked at her sternly. "Come clean, Polly. Why did you do it? Why did you mud yourself up before your class?"

Polly sniffed. "Why would I do a thing like that, Jack Russell?"

"Because you hate shows," I said.

"I like shows," said Polly. "If I win a ribbon Gloria Smote is pleased. I like to please Gloria Smote."

Jack's Facts.

Dogs don't do anything if there's nothing in it for them.
People sometimes do.
That makes dogs smarter than people.
This is a fact.

"How did you get mudded, then?" I demanded.

"I don't know," said Polly. "I didn't see."

"You must have smelled whoever it was. Dachs mightn't have superior super-sniffers like Jacks, but they can still sniff."

"A dach can sniff as well as any Jack," snapped Polly. "Tell me, Jack Russell. What can *your* superior super-sniffer sniff today?"

I sniff-sniffed as I tried to make a nose map.

Jack's map...

1. Dog and soap.

2. People and soap.

3. Biscuits and soap.

4. Mud and soap.

5. Soap.

"I see what you mean," I said. "The crime scene is contaminated by soap."

I went to interview more suspects. The mudded Dalmatians and the mudded schnauzers all told the same story. Shuffle the pug admitted that he hated shows, but he denied mudding himself in protest. His evidence agreed with Polly's. Someone had put mud on

him, but he hadn't noticed who. Hmm,
I thought. These dogs are not
pupetrators. These dogs are the victims
of a Phantom Mudder.

The schnauzer class finished, and the
loudhowler howled that the setters
would be judged after the squekes.

"Lordie? *Lordie?*" Caterina Smith was
yelling for Lord Red.

I'd sent Red to count mudded dogs,
but I'd already interviewed most of the
victims. Where was Red?

Foxie was sitting under Auntie
Tidge's chair, eating a special biscuit.
"Hey Foxie," I said. "Have you seen Red?"

"No," said Foxie. "I did see a black
setter though."

"Are you sure?"

Foxie licked his whiskers. "Hard to be

sure of anything with all this soap about."

Foxie was right. I was having a terrierable time detecting without the full use of my superior super-sniffer.

"There he goes again!" said Foxie, as a big black dog raced by.

"Jack – *Jack*!" barked the black setter. Then I knew it wasn't a black setter. It was Red.

The Phantom Mudder had struck again, and this time Red was the victim.

Jack's Facts.

Even superior super-sniffers become less reliable when affected by soap.
This is a fact.

Jack's Glossary

Pupetrators. *Perpetrators (another word for criminals) who happen to be pups or dogs.*

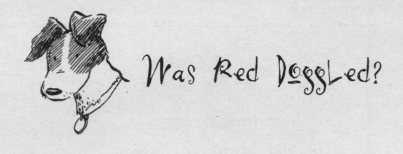

Was Red Doggled?

"Jack, Jack! I found eight mudded dogs!" Red wagged his tail, splattering me with mud. "Oops, make that nine!" spluttered Red.

"Ten," I said, glaring at Red.

"Eleven!" said Red, as a squeke yaffled by. It looked as if it had been dipped in melted doggy-choc. "Dora Barkins won't be pleased with that squeke," said Red. "Mudded squekes can't win ribbons and the squeke class is soon."

I didn't point out that mudded setters couldn't win ribbons either. I

didn't want to lead the witness.

"Do you know who mudded you?" I asked.

"Of course," said Red.

"You *do*?" Maybe Red wasn't as thick between the ears as I'd always thought.

"Of course I know," said Red.

"Who, then?" I asked doggedly. (You have to be dogged to get much sense out of Red.)

"The Phantom Mudder mudded me. Who else?"

I groaned.

With my lead witness a wash-out (and needing a wash), I tracked down a new line of enquiry.

Dog shows are about dogs, but the dogs weren't doing the mudding.

Dog shows are also about people.

Think, Jack, I told myself. Why would a person become a Phantom Mudder?

What if someone wanted his dog to win, and **doggled** the competition by mudding competing dogs? That would make sense if only one class had been doggled.

Someone with a dachshund might doggle Polly so his own dachshund

12

could win. But no-one would show a
dachshund, a schnauzer, a Dalmatian, a
pug, a squeke *and* a setter.

Besides, *all* the Dalmatians had been
mudded, so the whole class had been
cancelled. What was the use of doggling
them?

"Stand still," I said to Red. I summoned
up my superior super-sniffer.

"What do you sniff, Jack?" asked Red.

"Shush," I said. "I'm making a nose
map."

It didn't take long for me to nose
map Red.

Jack's map. . .

1. Soap and mud.

2. Soap, mud and Pooch Polish.

3. Soap, mud and more soap.

4. Soap, mud and biscuit.

"Did someone give you a biscuit today?" I asked Red.

Red looked shifty. "Caterina Smith says people at dog shows aren't allowed to give dogs biscuits."

I hoped Auntie Tidge didn't know that. She'd brought special biscuits for Foxie and me. "Why?"

"In case someone gets doggled by a biscuit with sleepy stuff in it."

I sniffed Red's face again. There was that faint hint of biscuit. . . It smelled like special biscuit.

Pause for thought. Could *Auntie Tidge* be the Phantom Mudder?

Dogwash! "Red," I said, "you're lying. Someone *did* give you a biscuit today. Who was it?"

Red looked embarrassed. "Nobody. I

mean, I only sort of found some."

"And did you sort of eat them?"

"Sort of," admitted Red. He put his nose down by mine. "A doggler would doggle the dog he wanted to doggle. He wouldn't leave doggled biscuits lying about for just anyone to eat."

"I'm not so sure," I said.

"Anyway, I wasn't doggled," said Red cheerfully. "I was only mudded." He cocked his head. "Caterina Smith is calling."

Red raced off, startling the mudded squeke as he went. Red was certain he hadn't been doggled.

I was certain he had.

I went back to Polly.

"Go away, Jack Russell," said Gloria Smote. "I don't want jack-lick on Polly."

I decided I *really* didn't like Gloria Smote.

"Polly, have you eaten a biscuit today?" I asked.

Polly licked her chops. "I'm not allowed to accept biscuits at dog shows."

"Thanks," I said to Polly. "That's all I need to know."

Jack's Facts.

Finding biscuits is not the same thing as accepting biscuits.
It is also not the same thing as stealing biscuits.
Anything left in reach of a dog is that dog's by right.
This **should** *be a fact.*

I asked a Dalmatian and one of the mudded schnauzers the same question I'd asked Red and Polly. I got the same result.

They said they had not accepted any biscuits from anyone today.

Neither of them actually said they hadn't *eaten* any biscuits. And when I pressed them, they admitted they had sort of found some biscuits. And sort of eaten them.

I knew in my bones that I was on the right track. I'd established the means of the crime. The Phantom Mudder was tempting dogs with biscuits, then mudding them while they ate.

That was the means. What about opportunity and motive?

Jack's Glossary.

Doggled. *Like nobbling a racehorse by doing something that will stop it from winning a race, but done to a dog.*

Foxie Foxes
the Judge

I sniff-sniffed about. I tracked down places where biscuits had been. I also discovered other mudded dogs.

The Phantom Mudder had struck again, and again.

I sniff-sniffed some more, and then I remembered something.

Judge Gibbs smelled of biscuits. Red called him "the biscuit man".

Maybe Judge Gibbs was the Phantom Mudder? He had the means. He had the biscuits.

"Why would Judge Gibbs mud a dog?" asked Foxie, when I told him my new theory. "Why would he mud dogs he's supposed to judge?"

"Maybe he likes small classes," I said. As I spoke, Judge Gibbs was judging five squekes. Three other entries had been mudded.

"But he wouldn't rather judge *no* class," snapped Foxie. "Remember the Dalmatians."

"**Bathwater!**" I said. "Those Dalmatians ruin my theory."

"Maybe Judge Gibbs just doesn't like Dalmatians," said Foxie.

"I wonder if Judge Gibbs likes fox terriers?" I suggested. "You go and **fox** him, Foxie. Pretend to be a very nice dog. See if he muds you."

"Why should I?" asked Foxie.

"He might give you a biscuit," I said.

"If so, bring it to me for **paw-rensic testing**."

Foxie is anyone's for a biscuit, so he trotted off to fox Judge Gibbs, who had just finished tying a ribbon on a squeke. I watched from behind a box of Pooch Polish.

<u>*Jack's Facts.*</u>

Pooch Polish is like soap.
Therefore, Pooch Polish should never be
used on a dog.
However, it is good to hide behind.
This is a fact.

Foxie began to fox Judge Gibbs. He pretended to be a very nice dog. He wagged his tail.

The judge bent and rubbed Foxie's ears. "Where did you spring from, Foxie?"

Foxie got up on his hind paws and sniffed Judge Gibbs's pocket. "Jack sent me to fox you," he yipped.

Judge Gibbs laughed. "Can you smell biscuits? I shouldn't give you one, you know. Not without asking your owner."

Sniff-sniff! went Foxie. He scraped Judge Gibbs's leg with one paw and whined. Then he did the **paw thing**. That was just the way I would have acted the part of a greedy dog. Only Foxie wasn't acting.

"Just one, then," said Judge Gibbs. "No more."

He took a special biscuit out of his pocket and gave it to Foxie. "Off you go, Foxie. It's almost time for me to judge the setter class."

I watched Foxie take the special biscuit in his jaws. I stared at Judge Gibbs. Would he mud Foxie? No, he just judged the setters.

Red wasn't with them. He was still being bathed by Caterina Smith.

Foxie came back to me. "Why are you

hiding behind the Pooch Polish box, Jack?"

"I was lying in wait while you foxed Judge Gibbs," I said. 'Where is that biscuit he gave you?'

"I ate it," said Foxie.

"I told you I wanted it for paw-rensic testing!"

"Well, I did some **jaw-rensic testing**," said Foxie. "It wasn't doggled."

Foxie was right. The judge hadn't mudded Foxie. How could he have been mudding dogs when he was judging? He had the means, and maybe a motive, but he had had no opportunity. That meant Judge "Biscuits" Gibbs was not the Phantom Mudder.

Who else would want to spoil the show?

Judge Gibbs, the dogs and the people

showing dogs were all eliminated as suspects. That left people *not* showing dogs!

How about Muddy Boots? He liked to wear mud on his boots. Sarge had said he couldn't show his biting bonehead. Muddy Boots had been angry about that.

Was Muddy Boots still at the dog show? I set out to investigate.

Jack's Glossary

Bathwater. *One of the worst swearwords I know.*

Foxed. *Fooled by a fox terrier.*

Paw-rensic testing. *Testing done by squashing suspect evidence with the paw.*

Paw thing. *Up on hind legs, paws held together as if praying. Means pleased excitement.*

Jaw-rensic testing. *Testing done by chewing.*

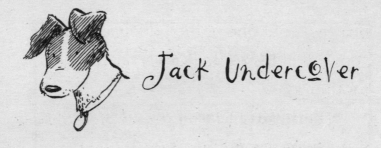

Jack Undercover

I found Muddy Boots with Mr
Latiman. The boneheads sat beside
them.

Sniff-sniffing gave me a good
whiff of Muddy Boots's boots. The
boots still had grey mud on them.
The mud on the mudded dogs had
been *black* mud.

So, Muddy Boots was not the
Phantom Mudder. The mud colour
was all wrong. "You're slack, Jack," I
said. "You should have thought of
that."

"Only a slack Jack would come

near *us*," said one of the boneheads. He showed all his teeth. "I see a terrier toothpick."

"*I* see a brainless bonehead," I said. I **jack-jumped** out of the way. I didn't want to be forced to hurt the bonehead.

I didn't wait about to investigate Mr Latiman. The Phantom Mudder had biscuits. If Mr Latiman had had biscuits, the boneheads would have swallowed them long ago.

I wasn't afraid of boneheads, of course. Any Jack is worth a dozen boneheads, and there were only four. All the same, I hurried back to Auntie Tidge, who was sitting with Dora Barkins and the squekes.

I settled down and chewed my **squeaker-bone**. It was lucky that Auntie

Tidge had brought it. I do my best thinking when I'm exercising my jaws.

As I chewed, Lord Red trotted up with Caterina Smith on the other end of a leash. Red was damp around the ears, but he looked quite cheerful.

Caterina Smith smiled at Auntie Tidge and Dora. "Are you enjoying the show?"

"Of course, dear," said Auntie Tidge. "Hello, Lordie."

Lord Red greeted Auntie Tidge. He put his paws around her neck and slurped his tongue up her cheek.

"Lordie, *no!*" snapped Caterina Smith. "I'm sorry," she said to Auntie Tidge.

Auntie Tidge hugged Red, then dried her face on her scarf. "I love dogs, and I'm used to Foxie-woxie and Jackie-wackie greeting me."

Foxie jumped up and greeted Auntie Tidge.

Caterina Smith sighed. "Lordie greeted Mrs Gibbs this morning. That woman *does* seem to have bad luck at shows. She's had her shoes chewed and her lipstick swallowed, and goodness knows what else. I wonder why she ever married a dog show judge if she doesn't like dogs?"

"Judge Gibbs has only been judging dog shows for a couple of years," said Dora Barkins. "He used to judge cat shows."

"I'd better get Lordie properly dry before the big dog class," said Caterina Smith. "Which class is next, Dora?"

Dora Barkins inspected her dog show

schedule. "It's the Shih tzu class next, and then small dogs."

Before they left, Lord Red put his nose down near mine. "You will catch the Phantom Mudder, Jack," said Red. "I know you will."

The loudhowler howled, "Shih tzu class!"

The Doggeroo Dog Show was almost over, and I still had the Mudder to catch.

I had been at the end of my tether, but now I had a new lead.

It was time for Jack Russell to go undercover as a show dog.

I chewed open a box of Pooch Polish, and rolled in it. I sneezed as I cleaned every toe.

I raced around the pavilion, giving

simple instructions to all the small dogs.
I instructed Polly, Jill Russell, the
squekes, and Shuffle the pug. I instructed
every small dog I could find.

"Beg for attention. Pretend to be cold.
Pretend to be frightened. Quiver and
quake. Shiver and shake. Yaffle and yip.
Do whatever it takes."

Did they do as they were told? Of
course they did! How could they disobey
a Jack on a mission?

Within minutes, half the people in
the Doggeroo Dog Show were cuddling

quivering, quaking, yaffling, yipping, shivering, shaking small dogs.

"What's wrong with them?" Dora Barkins wailed, as the squekes quivered and quaked.

"Don't worry, dear," said Auntie Tidge. "I expect they're just—"

I'm not sure what Auntie Tidge was planning to say, because Foxie jumped into her arms. It must have been his own idea. I hadn't instructed *him*.

It was time to bait the trap. The Shih tzu class would soon be over, so I had only a few minutes in which to get myself doggled and mudded.

I set off in search of the Phantom Mudder of Doggeroo.

Jack's Glossary

Jack-jump. *A very athletic spring done by a Jack Russell.*

Squeaker-bone. *Item for exercising teeth. Not to be confused with a toy.*

Splot

I was sure I had now identified the
Phantom Mudder, but I had to prove
it. I had to catch the Mudder in the
act. And that meant getting mudded.

I trotted about the pavilion,
looking as elegant as I could.

Come on Mudder, I thought.
You're not going to pass up a chance
to mud the only available small dog?

I trotted past Muddy Boots and
Mr Latiman. The boneheads sneered
at me. I trotted past Shuffle the pug,
snug in his person's arms. I trotted
past Caterina Smith and Lord Red.

And then I trotted past Sarge.

"Jack. Where are you off to?" asked Sarge. "You come back here!"

I trotted past High Heels, the woman Red had greeted. I trotted past Gloria Smote, who was cuddling Polly.

Then I trotted back the way I had come.

I had passed Gloria Smote and Polly when my super-sniffer detected soap and a hint of biscuit. Some dogs might have missed it, but you can't fool a tracking Jack with a superior super-sniffer. I spun around and sniffed.

There were two tiny biscuits lying on the ground.

I snapped one up, and subjected it to jaw-rensic testing. By the time I had tested the second one, a third one had appeared. Soon there was a fourth.

I ate my way along a trail of biscuits, and in behind a bale of hay. I was really getting into this undercover work. . .

Splot.

Suddenly I was under cover all right – under cover of a bucket of mud.

"Got you, dog!" The Phantom Mudder said it softly, but *nothing* has better ears than a Jack, even when the Jack is crunching biscuits and has mud in his lugs.

"No," I yapped, "I got *you!*" I let fly with the famous **jack-yap**. And then I jack-jumped right into the arms of. . .

Jack's Glossary

Jack-yap. *An especially piercing yap made by a Jack Russell.*

The Phantom Mudder Revealed

. . . the Phantom Mudder.

Between jack-yaps, I greeted her
several times.

I beat my tail. I flung my paws
around her. Then I slurped her cheek.

She tried to drop me, but I jack-
jumped up again, and clung with my
paws in her pockets.

Sarge heard my jack-yap and ran
to give me back-up. After him came
Foxie and Auntie Tidge, Red and
Caterina Smith and Judge Gibbs.

After *them*, came Polly and the
squekes, Gloria Smote, Dora Barkins,

Jill Russell, Shuffle and everyone else.

"What's going on?" asked Sarge sternly. (Sarge is good at being stern.)

Judge Gibbs stared at High Heels. "Katya! What's happened?"

"This *dog* has put mud all over me!" snarled High Heels. (That's right. The Phantom Mudder was Judge Gibbs's wife.)

"She mudded me first," I jack-yapped. "There is no doubt in my mind that she is the Phantom Mudder."

Sarge cleared his throat. "Mrs Gibbs, is that your bucket?" He pointed to the muddy bucket the Mudder had dropped when I jack-jumped up to Greet her.

"No, it's mine," said Judge Gibbs. "Katya, what have you *done*?"

Mrs Gibbs stamped her foot,

splashing mud over Sarge, Auntie Tidge
and Caterina Smith. "It's not fair!" she
said. "I hate dog shows. I've had my
shoes ruined, and my fingers bitten. I
had my gold lipstick eaten by a bulldog.
Today was the last straw." She pointed to
Red. "That setter spoiled my new coat
with mud, so I though I'd spoil a few
dog coats in revenge."

"But Katya, what did you hope to achieve?" said Judge Gibbs.

"I wanted to stop the show," said Katya Gibbs in a sulky voice. "Give me a cat show any day! *Cats* don't chew my shoes and eat my lipsticks and wipe mud all over my coat." She glared at Sarge. "But you didn't stop the show, did you? You just moved the muddy dogs into other classes!"

That's how Jack Russell, Dog Detective, solved the case of the Phantom Mudder. My superior super-sniffer wasn't at its best that day, so I had to rely on other methods of detection.

1. I eliminated suspects like dogs, their people, Judge Gibbs, Mr Latiman and Muddy Boots.

2. I took the suspect's motive into account. She'd told Caterina Smith how lots of dogs had bothered her at shows. Mr Latiman said Muddy Boots's dog had bitten the judge's wife the year before.

3. I took means and opportunity and evidence into account. High Heels could have got biscuits from Judge Gibbs. She had a show schedule, so she'd know just which dogs to mud before their classes. She always smelled of soap because she washed her hands every time she mudded a dog.

4. Finally, I took character into account. High Heels trod on Red's tail. Then she almost trod on Foxie and me. Finally, she called me a *sweet little*

doggie. No innocent person would insult a Jack like that.

What happened afterwards?

The show went on, of course. Polly won the small dog class. Red won the big dog class.

Auntie Tidge got the Phantom Mudder a cup of tea and an **unspecial biscuit**.

Sarge banned the Phantom Mudder from ever going to dog shows. He said she should go to every cat show instead.

Auntie Tidge gave Foxie and me special biscuits.

And what was my reward for solving the case of the Phantom Mudder?

That's right.

You guessed.

I got another bath.

Jack's Glossary.

Unspecial biscuit. *The kind of biscuit people eat.*

Jack Russell:

Keep track of all Jack's cases...

Jack Russell:
The detective with a nose for crime

Dognapped!

Jack's squeaker bone has been snatched! Is he in danger of being dognapped?

Jack Russell:
The detective with a nose for crime
Pug in Trouble

Shuffle the Pug's collar has been stolen – and dogs without collars go to the dogs' home! It's time for Jack to race to the rescue...

Jack Russell:

Dognapped!

An extract...

I woke when the birds started singing. I got out of my basket, trotted across the grass and did what dogs do.

Then I checked my nose map.

Sniff-sniff. Sparrows-under-the-tree scent.

Sniff-sniff. Cat-crossed-the-lawn-last-night scent.

Sniff-sniff. Old-boot scent.

Sniff-sniff. . .

Something was wrong. I *sniff-sniffed* back a few paces. Old-boot scent. But the boot was not there.

Very strange. Very odd. Sparrows move. Cats move. Boots don't move. But why should I care? An old boot had been in my new garden. Now it wasn't. Not my problem.

I scratched at the door and yapped until Sarge let me in.

Jack's facts.

_Scratching and yapping gets you into
the house when you're out.
Scratching and yapping gets you out
of the house when you're in.
This is a fact._

I had breakfast while Sarge got ready for work. I thought about hiding in the house. Then I remembered Sarge would be gone all morning.

I followed him outside.

"See you at lunchtime, Jack!" said Sarge.

I went back to my basket.

That's when I discovered a crime had been committed.

Someone had stolen my squeaker-bone!

<u>*Jack's facts.*</u>

When someone takes an old boot,
*that's **not** my problem.*
When someone takes my squeaker-bone,
*that **is** my problem.*
This is a fact.

I sniff-searched my basket. I sniff-searched the porch. I sniff-searched the yard. No squeaker-bone. I sniff-searched again. No old boot. No squeaker-bone.

This was serious! There was a crime wave in Doggeroo! I was glad Sarge would soon be home.

Sarge is a police detective. If someone does something bad, Sarge investigates. He finds out who did it. He finds out why they did it. He finds out how they did it. Then he stops them from doing it again.

Sarge could find out who took my squeaker-bone. He could make them give it back. When Sarge came home for lunch, I laid a complaint. I grabbed his trouser leg. I tugged him towards my basket.

"No time for games now, Jack," said Sarge.

I pawed at his leg. Sarge tramped out the gate.

Sarge wasn't going to investigate the theft. Someone else would have to take the case.

Someone like: Jack Russell, Dog Detective.

Sarge could find out who took my squeaker-bone. He could make them give it back. When Sarge came home for lunch, I laid a complaint. I grabbed his trouser leg. I tugged him towards my basket.

"No time for games now, Jack," said Sarge.

I pawed at his leg. Sarge tramped out the gate.

Sarge wasn't going to investigate the theft. Someone else would have to take the case.

Someone like: Jack Russell, Dog Detective.